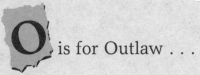

O is for Outlaw . . .

Just as Ruth Rose picked up her backpack, they heard Dink's uncle shout.

The kids ran down the hall and practically bumped into Uncle Warren. His face was white, and he looked sick.

"The . . . the painting," Dink's uncle stammered. "Someone's stolen Forest's painting!"

Dink looked past his uncle into the study. The painting was gone.

This book is dedicated to my parents,
Leo "Zeke" Roy and Marie Jeanne Roy.
—R.R.

For Arthur Davis, a big A to Z fan
—J.S.G.

Text copyright © 2001 by Ron Roy
Cover art copyright © 2015 by Stephen Gilpin
Interior illustrations copyright © 2001 by John Steven Gurney

All rights reserved. Published in the United States by Random House Children's Books, a division of Random House LLC, a Penguin Random House Company, New York. Originally published in paperback by Random House Children's Books, New York, in 2001.

Random House and the colophon and A to Z Mysteries are registered trademarks and A Stepping Stone Book and the colophon and the A to Z Mysteries colophon are trademarks of Random House LLC.

Visit us on the Web!
SteppingStonesBooks.com
randomhousekids.com

Educators and librarians, for a variety of teaching tools, visit us at RHTeachersLibrarians.com

Library of Congress Cataloging-in-Publication Data
Roy, Ron.
The orange outlaw / by Ron Roy ; illustrated by John Steven Gurney.
p. cm. — (A to Z mysteries)
"A Stepping Stone book."
Summary: While visiting Dink's uncle in New York City, Dink, Josh, and Ruth Rose help uncover who is responsible for stealing a very valuable painting.
ISBN 978-0-375-80270-6 (trade) — ISBN 978-0-375-90270-3 (lib. bdg.) —
ISBN 978-0-307-53938-0 (ebook)
[1. Art thefts—Fiction. 2. Mystery and detective stories.] I. Gurney, John, ill. II. Title. III. Series:
Roy, Ron. A to Z mysteries.
PZ7.R8139 Or 2001 [Fic]—dc21 2001019415

Printed in the United States of America
33 32 31 30 29 28 27

This book has been officially leveled by using the F&P Text Level Gradient™ Leveling System.

Random House Children's Books supports the First Amendment and celebrates the right to read.

A to Z Mysteries®

The Orange Outlaw

by **Ron Roy**

illustrated by
John Steven Gurney

A STEPPING STONE BOOK™

Random House 🏠 New York

CHAPTER 1

Dink, Josh, and Ruth Rose stood on Uncle Warren's balcony. Nine floors below, the cars, buses, and taxis of New York City zoomed by.

As dusk turned to night, the city's lights began to blink on. People were strolling to restaurants and theaters.

Dink's uncle stepped onto the balcony. "That's a pretty sight, isn't it?" he said.

"It's great," Dink said. "I feel like an eagle up here."

"Thanks for inviting us for the weekend," Josh told him.

"You are entirely welcome, my boy," Uncle Warren said.

"And thanks for inviting us to your block party," Ruth Rose said. "I've never been to one before."

Josh let out a chuckle. "My little brothers have block parties all the time," he said. "They bring their blocks out to the sandbox and throw them at each other."

Uncle Warren laughed. "In New York City, we often have parties where everyone on the block is invited," he explained. "Tonight we plan to raise money for the Central Park Zoo."

"Why does the zoo need money?" asked Ruth Rose.

"Some of the animals need more space," Uncle Warren said.

"Can they make all that money from one party?" Josh asked, gazing down at the street.

"Tonight is just the beginning," Uncle Warren said. "The zoo will be raising money for at least a year."

He looked at his watch. "We'd better get going. But first, I want to show you something."

The kids followed Dink's uncle through the living room to a small study at the back of the apartment. The room held a desk, a chair, and tall shelves crammed with books.

On the desk lay a painting of a rowboat floating on a pond.

"Do you like it?" Uncle Warren asked.

"It's pretty," Ruth Rose said. "I like the flowers on the water."

"Those are lily pads," Uncle Warren

said. "This was painted a long time ago by a man named Claude Monet. It's very valuable."

"Is the painting yours?" Dink asked.

"I wish it were, Donny," his uncle said. "My friend Forest Evans just bought it vacationing in France. He shipped it to me for safekeeping. He'll collect this beauty when he returns to New York in a couple of days."

Uncle Warren looked at his watch. "It's time to go downstairs," he said. "Help me shut off a few lights."

The kids walked around switching off lights.

"Leave the one over the kitchen table on!" Dink's uncle called.

In the kitchen, a hanging light shone down on a wooden bowl filled with oranges. Dink was tempted to take one but decided to wait till later.

They left the apartment and Uncle Warren locked the door. Then they crossed the hall and crowded into the small elevator. Dink pushed the button that said LOBBY.

"What happens to all the cars when you have a block party?" Josh asked as they rode down.

"The police seal off the street," Uncle Warren explained. "You'll see."

A minute later, they left the elevator, crossed the lobby, and walked to the front door.

"Hello, kids," said Roger, the doorman. He looked like royalty in his crisp uniform and pointy mustache. "The block party sure has drawn a lot of people!"

"Are you going?" Ruth Rose asked him.

He shook his head. "Afraid not, missy. I have to stay at the door. But I'll be able to see a lot from here. Have fun! I hear there'll be lots of good stuff to eat."

"Awesome!" Josh said, rubbing his belly.

"Still hungry, Josh?" Uncle Warren asked. "Didn't I feed you enough?"

Josh grinned. "That was two hours ago!"

"Josh is like a baby wolf," Ruth Rose said. "He needs to eat ten times a day."

The kids and Uncle Warren walked outside.

It was a warm night in June, and the street was crowded. Music, voices, and food smells filled the air.

"This is so cool, Uncle Warren," Dink said. "We're standing right where cars and buses usually drive!"

"Yes," Uncle Warren said, "and tomorrow morning, they'll be back."

"Evening, Mr. Duncan," a woman

behind them said. She was stooped and
had a lined face and wild orange hair.

"Hello, Miss Booker," Uncle Warren
said. "You haven't met my nephew
Donny and his friends, have you? Kids,
Miss Booker is the building manager."

The kids each said hello and shook
Miss Booker's hand. She was wearing a
raincoat even though the sky was clear.

"A pleasure," the woman said. "Enjoy the party."

She turned around and entered the building. Through the glass door, Dink saw her talk to Roger. After a minute, she walked toward the elevator.

"What does a building manager do?" Josh asked.

"Many things," Uncle Warren said. "She fixes leaky faucets, calls electricians, and makes sure the building is kept clean. She'll even deliver packages to my door so Roger doesn't have to leave his station."

"Does she live here, like you?" Ruth Rose asked.

Uncle Warren nodded. "Miss Booker has a small apartment in the basement," he said.

Suddenly, Josh stopped dead in his tracks. "You guys aren't gonna believe this," he said, "but I just saw a flying watermelon!"

CHAPTER 2

Josh led the group over to a guy juggling fruit. Big fruit! A watermelon, a grapefruit, a cantaloupe, and a pineapple circled through the air over the man's head.

"My mother would tell him not to play with his food," Josh whispered.

A boy a little taller than Dink stood in front of the man. "Ready, Dad?" he asked.

When the man nodded, the kid tossed a bunch of bananas into the air.

Everyone watching said, "Oooooh!"

as the bananas joined the rest of the fruit.

Not far from the juggler, the kids noticed a man in a hat and vest leading a pony around a ring. Suddenly, an orangutan dressed as a clown leaped onto the pony. The ape stood on his head as the pony galloped faster and faster.

While everyone cheered, a woman also wearing a hat and vest passed out flyers. Dink took one and stuck it in his pocket.

The man clapped his hands, and the pony jumped into a trailer with the ape still on its back.

Josh started down the street. "Look at the dummy!" he said.

"Takes one to know one," Dink said, grinning at Josh.

"I think he means the *wooden* one," Ruth Rose said.

On a small stage sat a man with a wooden doll on his lap. The two were talking to each other.

"I'm hungry!" the dummy said. His hinged mouth opened and closed as he spoke, and his bright eyes moved from side to side.

"Go to sleep," the man answered in a deeper voice.

"Feed me, or I'll report you for dummy abuse!" the dummy said.

"How do they do that?" Josh asked. The man's voice seemed to be coming out of the dummy's mouth.

The man pulled a cookie from an open bag at his feet. He grinned at the audience and ate it.

"Hey, gimme one of those!" his dummy yelled.

"No."

"Yes!"

"No," the man said. "You've already had dessert."

"Gimme a cookie, or I stop talking," the dummy said.

The audience laughed.

The man sighed and rolled his eyes. "Oh, all right. But just one."

The man reached down and took a second cookie from the bag. He put it in the dummy's mouth. "There, happy now?"

The dummy chewed, swallowed, and burped. The audience loved it. "Thank you," the dummy said to the man.

"You're welcome," the man said. Holding the dummy in his arms, he stood up and bowed.

"Hey, mister. Where'd that cookie go?" Josh called out.

The man smiled at Josh. "Down into his wooden tummy!"

Josh laughed. He turned to Dink, Ruth Rose, and Uncle Warren. "That dummy made me hungry," he said.

"How about some pizza?" Uncle Warren asked. "I think I noticed a vendor selling slices."

The four walked to the pizza stand and bought slices. They ate them as they enjoyed more of the block party.

When Dink started yawning, his uncle led the group back to the building. Roger was standing just inside the lobby door.

"Did you have a good time?" he asked.

"It was great," Dink said.

"I think the evening will be a big success," Uncle Warren said. "Good night, Roger."

"I sure hope so," Roger said. "Night, Mr. Duncan."

Uncle Warren pushed the button to call the elevator. A minute later, they entered his apartment.

"Why don't you kids get ready for bed, and then we can see what's on TV?" he suggested, heading for his study.

Just as Ruth Rose picked up her backpack, they heard Dink's uncle shout.

The kids ran down the hall and practically bumped into Uncle Warren. His face was white, and he looked sick.

"Uncle Warren, what's the matter?" Dink asked.

"The . . . the painting," Dink's uncle stammered. "Someone's stolen Forest's painting!"

CHAPTER 3

Dink looked past his uncle into the study. The painting was gone.

"I've got to call the police," Uncle Warren said. He hurried toward the kitchen, leaving the kids standing in the hallway.

"Who could have taken it?" Ruth Rose asked.

"And how?" wondered Josh. "The door was locked."

"Kids, come quickly!" Dink's uncle yelled from the other end of the apartment.

They ran back down the hallway and into the kitchen.

"Look at *that*!" Uncle Warren said, pointing at the kitchen table.

The tabletop was littered with orange juice and peels. The fruit bowl was overturned. More peels and dribbles of juice covered the floor.

"Yuck, it's all sticky!" Josh said, backing away from a small puddle.

"This is terrible!" Uncle Warren said as he called the police.

"Guys, look!" Ruth Rose was

pointing to an orange peel near the balcony.

The kids walked over, and Ruth Rose opened the balcony door. "There's juice on the door handle, too," she said, wiping her hand on her jeans.

They found more orange peels on the balcony.

"Guy must've been hungry," Josh observed.

Dink looked down over the balcony railing. "Could this be how the thief got into the apartment?" he asked.

"How?" Josh asked. "On a hang glider? Dink, we're ten stories up, remember?"

Uncle Warren joined them. "A detective will be here soon," he said. Then he noticed the orange peels all over the balcony. "Goodness!"

The kids started to pick up the orange peels.

"Leave them," Uncle Warren said.

"The police said not to touch anything."

They walked into the living room and sat down to wait.

"Forest will be devastated," Uncle Warren said. "Thank goodness he had the painting insured! At least he'll get his money back."

Suddenly, Roger's voice came over the small speaker next to the door. "Mr. Duncan, there's a detective here to see you. Shall I send him up?"

Uncle Warren jumped up and ran to the door. Pressing the TALK button on the speaker, he said, "Thank you, Roger." Then he opened the door and walked into the hall.

The kids sat on the sofa staring at the front door. After a few moments, they heard the elevator door open. Dink's uncle said, "Yes, this is the place. I'm Warren Duncan."

Uncle Warren walked back in, followed by a tall man wearing a dark suit and tie.

"Kids, this is Detective Frank Costello," Dink's uncle said.

The man nodded at the kids, then looked around the room. He had black eyes, dark, swept-back hair, and a nose that looked as if it had been broken.

"Where was the painting?" Detective Costello asked.

"Back here," Uncle Warren said, leading him down the hall toward the study.

"Let's go talk to Roger," Ruth Rose said.

"Why?" asked Josh.

"Maybe he saw someone sneaking around," she answered.

"Good idea," Dink said. He grabbed a pad and scribbled a note to his uncle. "Okay, let's go." He and Josh followed Ruth Rose to the elevator.

In the lobby, they found Roger at his desk near the front door. Through the glass, Dink could see that the block party was winding down.

"Going out again?" Roger asked the kids.

Dink shook his head. "Someone stole a valuable painting from my uncle's apartment!" he said.

Roger jumped from his seat. "A theft in our building? I can't believe it!"

"It happened while we were at the block party," Josh said. "The creep ate all the oranges, too!"

"We were wondering if you noticed anyone strange," Ruth Rose put in.

Roger shook his head. "I was here the entire time and saw only people who live here," he said. "Absolutely no one else. . . ."

Roger closed his eyes, then opened them slowly. "I just remembered. Mrs. Cornelius on the ninth floor called down about an hour ago. She thought she saw someone on her balcony. I offered to go up and check, but she said not to bother."

"Is her balcony below Dink's uncle's?" Ruth Rose asked.

Roger nodded. "All the balconies on the rear of the building are directly above or below each other."

Ruth Rose looked at Dink and Josh. "Then maybe she saw the thief!"

CHAPTER 4

Dink explained about the orange peels they'd found on his uncle's balcony.

Roger shook his head. "But how would a thief climb the building?" he asked.

"Why don't we go outside and take a look?" Josh suggested. "Maybe we'll find a clue."

"Kids, it's pretty late," Roger said. "Perhaps you should wait till tomorrow. . . ."

"We'll only stay a minute," Dink said.

"Well, okay." Roger directed them to

a metal door around the corner from the elevator.

Dink slid back a long bolt and shoved the door open. They walked out into a narrow, well-lit space behind the building. It was completely enclosed except for an alley that led to the street. Next to the building, a Dumpster sat in the shadows.

"I wonder," Ruth Rose said, staring at the Dumpster. "What if the thief climbed on top of that? Could he reach the first balcony?"

Dink stared up. "The first two floors don't have balconies," he observed. "Even standing on the Dumpster, I don't see how the crook could have gotten up or down this way."

"Then he had to go through the front door," Josh said. "But if Roger didn't see him . . ."

Just then, an angry voice came out of the darkness. "What are you doing back here? This is private property!"

"Who . . . who's there?" Dink asked.

A figure walked out of the shadows. It was Miss Booker. She didn't look happy to see them.

"It's just us," Dink said. "My uncle is Mr. Duncan. We met you at the block party earlier tonight."

The woman stopped a few feet from the kids. Her hands were jammed into her coat pockets. She wore a cap pulled down over her orange hair. "Why are you kids out here?" she asked.

"There was a robbery in my uncle's apartment," Dink said.

Miss Booker nodded. "I know. Roger just told me."

"We thought the crook might have come this way," Ruth Rose said.

"Yeah," Josh said, "except he'd have to have wings."

Miss Booker looked up the side of the building. She touched the bricks with a long finger. "A few years ago, I could've climbed this no problem," she said.

The kids stared at the woman.

Miss Booker smiled. "When I was your age, my father and mother owned a carnival. My brothers did the high-wire act. They were known as the Flying Bookers. I was the girl on the trapeze."

"Um, did you happen to see anyone in the alley?" Dink asked.

Miss Booker shook her head. "The alley was blocked off," she said.

"Blocked off? How?" Ruth Rose asked.

"I'll show you." The kids followed Miss Booker down the alley toward the front of the building.

"Right here," Miss Booker said, stopping where the alley met the street. "There was a trailer parked here during the block party."

"A trailer?" Dink asked, trying to remember.

Just then, Roger opened the front door and leaned out. "Donald, your uncle wants you and your friends to come upstairs," he said.

"Okay, we'll be right in," Dink said. "Good night, Miss Booker. Maybe we'll see you tomorrow."

"Maybe you will," the woman said. Then she turned and walked back down the dark alley.

CHAPTER 5

When the kids stepped out of the elevator, Uncle Warren was waiting in the hallway. "Thank you for leaving me a note, but it's past your bedtime, Donny."

"Is the detective still here?" Dink asked.

"No, he left a few minutes ago," his uncle said. "He checked for fingerprints and took samples of the orange peels and juice."

They walked into the kitchen. The orange peels were gone, but the floor was still sticky. Patches of white fingerprint powder made blotches on the counter and kitchen table. The empty fruit bowl was in the sink.

"Do you know Mrs. Cornelius?" Dink asked his uncle.

Uncle Warren smiled. "A lot of people know Corinne Cornelius," he said. "She was a Broadway actress years ago. She lives in the apartment right below this one. We have tea together all the time. Why do you ask?"

Dink told his uncle what they'd learned from Roger. "Mrs. Cornelius might have seen the thief on her balcony," he said. "Maybe she can tell us what he looks like!"

"Donny, Mrs. Cornelius is quite old," his uncle said. "And I'm afraid her eyesight is failing."

Uncle Warren looked around his kitchen and sighed. "I should clean up, but I'm exhausted. This mess will have to wait till morning," he said. "Now off to bed, kiddos."

"We'll help you tomorrow," Ruth Rose said.

"Thank you, my dear. Sweet dreams, everyone," Uncle Warren said as he padded toward his bedroom.

"I don't know about you guys," Ruth Rose said, "but I couldn't sleep a wink right now."

"Me either," Dink said. The three headed for the living room. Ruth Rose sat next to Dink on the sofa, and Josh plopped down on the carpet.

"I've been thinking," Ruth Rose said. "How many people knew your uncle had a valuable painting in his apartment?"

"Roger might have known about it," Dink said.

Josh sat up. "Of course!" he said. "*Roger's* the crook!"

"But he was at the door all night," Dink said.

"That's what he told us," Ruth Rose said. "He could have been lying. Does Roger have the key to this apartment?"

"Guys, my uncle and Roger are friends," Dink protested. "Plus, he's worked in this building for ages."

"Don't you watch TV?" Josh asked, wiggling his eyebrows up and down. "The butler—I mean, the doorman—did it!"

Dink laughed. "You're crazy. No way Roger snuck up here and stole that painting."

Josh got up and walked into the kitchen. Dink heard the refrigerator door open and close.

"Well, who else knew about it?" Ruth Rose asked.

"How about Miss Booker?" Josh said when he came back. He was carrying a handful of grapes. "She told us she used to swing on a trapeze. Maybe she climbs buildings now. Plus, she knew we were all out of the apartment during the block party."

Ruth Rose nodded. "She's the building manager, so I'll bet she has keys to all the apartments. She wouldn't *have* to climb the building!"

"But how would she know my uncle even had the painting?" Dink asked.

"Dink, remember your uncle said one of Miss Booker's jobs is delivering packages?" Ruth Rose said. "Maybe she brought the painting up to your uncle. He might have told her what was inside the wrapping."

"And she might have told Roger," Josh said. "Heck, maybe they did it together. Roger could've been the lookout while she was up here stealing the painting!"

"And tossing orange peels all over the place?" Dink said. "Wouldn't that be kind of dumb?"

"Maybe she did that on purpose," Ruth Rose said. "Leaving orange peels on the balcony would make it look like the crook climbed down the building."

"Yeah," Josh said, "and that would make us think it was someone who *didn't* have keys."

"Okay, but what about the juice all over the kitchen?" Dink asked. "Why would Miss Booker do that?"

"Easy," Josh said, "she wanted to confuse the cops."

Dink yawned, then stood up and stretched. "Well, whoever it was did a good job confusing *me*!"

He walked out to the balcony and looked up at the stars. High in the sky, he made out the blinking lights on an airplane. He wondered where the plane was coming from.

Josh and Ruth Rose came and stood next to him.

"I thought of someone else who might have known about the painting," Ruth Rose said.

"Who?" Dink asked.

"Mrs. Cornelius," she answered.

Dink stared at her. "But she's old and can't see well," he said. "My uncle told us that a little while ago."

"He also told us she used to be an *actress*," Ruth Rose said.

"Besides," Josh added, "you don't need perfect eyesight to steal a painting."

"But if Mrs. Cornelius is the crook, why would she tell Roger she saw someone on her balcony?"

"Maybe she did it to keep anyone from suspecting her," Ruth Rose said.

Dink thought for a moment. "Okay, but how would she get into my uncle's apartment? Or are you going to tell me she swung up on a vine, like Tarzan?"

Josh laughed. "I don't know. Maybe she stole a spare key when she was here having tea," he said. "But I say we go have a talk with Mrs. Cornelius tomorrow morning."

CHAPTER 6

"Josh, wake up."

Dink shook Josh's shoulder, then yanked the covers off him. "Come on, help me clean the kitchen before my uncle gets up."

Josh mumbled something and pulled the covers back over himself.

"He made us breakfast . . . ," Dink said.

Josh shot out of the bed, tripping over his sneakers as he charged into the kitchen.

Ruth Rose was already there, washing the fruit bowl.

"I don't see any food," Josh grumbled.

"No, but you will after we get this mess cleaned up," Dink told him. "Blueberry pancakes are my uncle's specialty."

Josh dropped into a chair. "I've been lied to," he mumbled.

"Come on, Josh," Dink said. "If we work together, we can have this done in ten minutes."

"I'll wash the floor," Ruth Rose said, dragging a mop from a closet.

Dink handed Josh a damp sponge. "While you're sitting there, wipe the chairs and tabletop."

"I thought we were going to talk to Mrs. Cornelius this morning," Josh said, giving the table a fast swipe.

"We are." Dink opened his uncle's address book. "I'm calling her right now."

When Dink had Mrs. Cornelius on the line, he introduced himself and asked if they could visit her for a few minutes. He thanked her and hung up.

"We can go down as soon as we're done cleaning up," he said. "Let's get to work!"

Dink turned the radio on low, and they cleaned to country songs.

"Hey, look what I found!" Josh said. He held up a long orange hair. "It was caught on the back of this chair."

Dink and Ruth Rose walked over and studied the hair. "Looks like one of yours, Josh," Ruth Rose said.

"Is not," Josh said. "My hair is red, not this orange color. And mine's a *lot* cleaner!"

Ruth Rose took the hair and held it up to the light. "Miss Booker has orange hair," she said.

"We can check her out later," Dink said. He folded the hair inside a paper towel and stuck it in his pocket. "Let's finish up and go see Mrs. Cornelius."

Ten minutes later, the kids quietly left the apartment. They found the stairs and walked down one floor. Dink knocked on Mrs. Cornelius's door.

It was opened by a woman who had white hair and was wearing a fuzzy robe. Behind thick eyeglasses, her pale blue eyes looked huge.

"Good morning!" Mrs. Cornelius chirped. "I see I'm not the only one who likes to get up with the birds. Come in, come in!"

Using a cane, she led them into a cheerful living room. "Please sit on the sofa, where I can see you," she said.

The kids lined up on the sofa. Mrs. Cornelius sat opposite them. She leaned close and studied their faces.

"Now tell me why three children have come to visit an old lady like me," she said.

Dink told Mrs. Cornelius about the stolen painting.

"Goodness!" she said. "I always miss the excitement. When did it happen, dear?"

"Last night, during the block party," Ruth Rose said.

Mrs. Cornelius clapped her hands.

"That prowler I saw on my balcony must have been the thief!" she said. "I'm a witness!"

"Um, we were wondering if you could tell us what happened."

Using her cane for support, Mrs. Cornelius stood up. "Come with me." She walked to her balcony. "Pull those drapes, dear," she said to Josh.

When the drapes were opened, the kids looked out onto the balcony. It was just like Uncle Warren's, except that several bird feeders were attached to the balcony railing.

"I love to feed the birds, but I have trouble seeing them," Mrs. Cornelius said. "That's why I bought this!"

She pointed to a round magnifying glass about the size of a pie plate. It was stuck to the inside of the balcony's glass door.

Dink looked curiously through the

magnifying glass. "Wow, everything looks bigger!" he said.

"Isn't it fun?" Mrs. Cornelius said. "I heard a noise last night, so I walked over and peeked through the drapes. Someone was on the balcony!"

"What did he look like?" Dink asked.

"I thought you'd never ask," Mrs. Cornelius said. She took a pad out of the pocket of her robe and handed it to Dink.

Written in large, spidery letters were the words:

a baggy coat
very poor posture
wrinkled face

Dink gulped when he read the last two words:

orange hair

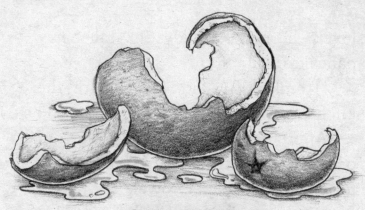

CHAPTER 7

"Still think the crook is Mrs. Cornelius?" Dink asked as they walked back up to the tenth floor.

"Mrs. Cornelius's description sure does sound like Miss Booker," Ruth Rose admitted.

Dink laughed. "Bad posture, baggy clothes, orange hair—sounds more like Josh!"

He opened the door to his uncle's apartment.

"There you are," Uncle Warren said. "Thank you for cleaning up. What a lovely surprise! Ready for blueberry pancakes?"

"I am!" Josh said, heading for the kitchen.

After taking his first bite of pancake, Dink reached into his pocket for the folded paper towel. He pulled out the orange hair and showed it to his uncle.

"Josh found this stuck to one of the chairs," he said. "We think it came from the crook."

Dink's uncle studied the hair. "This is odd-looking. Wait, I'll be back in a jiffy," he said.

The kids heard cupboard doors opening and closing. A minute later, Dink's uncle was back, carrying a small wooden box.

He moved the pancake platter to one side and set the box in its place. Then he pulled off the lid, revealing a shiny microscope. He plugged the microscope's cord into a wall outlet.

"Josh, may I have one of your hairs?" he asked.

"Sure." Josh grimaced as he yanked out a hair. Then he passed the hair to Uncle Warren.

Dink's uncle laid both hairs on a glass slide, then placed the slide under the microscope lens. He adjusted the scope and put one eye to it.

"Well, I think it's a real hair," Uncle Warren said after a minute. "But it's very different from yours, Josh. Take a look. Your hair is the one on the right."

Josh bent over the scope. "All I see is nothing," he said.

"Try closing one eye," Uncle Warren said.

"Wow, that's better!" Josh said. "The hairs look like tree trunks!"

Ruth Rose was next. "The hairs do look different," she said. "Look, Dink."

Dink closed one eye and peered

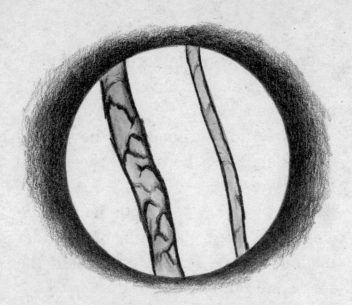

through the lens. The hair on the right
was thin and smooth-looking. The one
on the left was fatter and more orange
than the other one.

"Mrs. Cornelius told us she saw
someone on her balcony with orange
hair," Dink said.

"She did?" Uncle Warren said.

Ruth Rose nodded. "She has this
neat magnifying glass attached to her
balcony door," she said. "So she can
watch the birds at her feeders."

"I looked through it," Dink told his

uncle. "It makes stuff look bigger and clearer." He told his uncle how Mrs. Cornelius had described the person on her balcony.

"Baggy coat and poor posture? Well, well. Maybe she really did see our thief!" Uncle Warren said. "I'd better call Detective Costello."

While his uncle dialed the phone, Dink motioned for Josh and Ruth Rose to follow him. They left the apartment, but Dink walked past the elevator.

"Where are we going?" Josh asked. "I wanted a few more of those pancakes."

"Let's walk down," Dink said, shoving open the exit door. "I don't want anyone to see us."

"See us what?" Ruth Rose asked.

"I want to get one of Miss Booker's hairs," Dink said. "And I don't want Roger to see us, just in case they're partners."

"So now you think they did it together?" Josh asked.

"I don't know, but we can't take any chances," Dink said.

"Oh, boy," Josh said, skipping down the stairs.

Dink and Ruth Rose followed Josh. "How do you plan to get a hair?" Ruth Rose asked.

Dink shrugged. "I don't know yet," he admitted.

Out of breath, the kids finally reached the lobby. Dink peeked around the corner to make sure Roger wasn't watching; then they hurried out the rear exit.

They didn't see Miss Booker behind the building. Josh took a look down the alley, but she wasn't there either.

"Let's look out front," Ruth Rose suggested.

Dink and Josh followed Ruth Rose

down the alley. They were halfway to the front of the building when Ruth Rose bent down and picked something off the ground.

Dink and Josh caught up and looked over her shoulder.

Ruth Rose was holding a Polaroid snapshot. It was a picture of a framed painting.

Dink gasped when he recognized the rowboat floating on a pond.

"It's a picture of the stolen painting!" he said.

CHAPTER 8

In the photograph, the painting stood on a table. Part of a window was also visible, with buildings in the distance.

Josh asked, "What's this doing in the alley?"

"I think I know," Ruth Rose said. "The thief must have used this picture to identify the painting. After he stole it, he threw the picture away."

"If the thief tossed the picture here, that means he probably *did* climb down the balconies," Dink said.

"You mean *she*," Josh said.

Ruth Rose shook her head. "But if Miss Booker did it," she asked, "why would she tell us she can climb buildings? Wouldn't that just point the finger at her?"

"Maybe she's giving us false clues," Josh said. "She tells us she can climb the building and drops this picture in the alley. But all the time, she probably just went through the front door with her key."

"No matter who stole the painting," Dink said, "the crook's fingerprints should be on this picture." He carefully slipped the snapshot inside his shirt. "We have to show it to my uncle!"

The kids ran down the alley to the front of the building. Weekend traffic whizzed by. A few people hurried toward the subway stop. A man in gray work clothes was sweeping up litter.

A mound of litter stood at the

entrance to the alley. As the kids walked past, Josh accidentally kicked the pile.

"Hey, watch your step there, young fella," said the man with the broom.

"Sorry," Josh said, stepping away from the litter. Using his foot, he scraped the stuff back together.

Then he knelt down and picked something out of the debris. "Hey, guys, look!" Josh held up an orange peel.

The man with the broom chuckled. "There was a block party here last night," he said. "A guy had a trailer with an orangutan and a pony parked right here. Man, that orangutan sure ate a lot of oranges!"

Dink took the peel from Josh and looked at it carefully. Caught in the peel was a long orange hair.

Ruth Rose peered over Dink's shoulder. "It's just like the hair Josh found in the kitchen!" she said.

Josh looked back up the alley. "Guys," he said, "Miss Booker didn't climb up those balconies. That orangutan did!"

Ruth Rose's eyes grew wide. "Orangutans *are* great climbers!" she said.

"And they have long orange hair and eat fruit!" said Josh.

Dink stared at Josh and Ruth Rose. "You mean you think the orangutan is the thief?"

"Why not?" Josh said. "People train orangutans to do all kinds of stuff. Why couldn't one be taught to steal a painting?"

Dink tapped the snapshot inside his shirt. "If you're right, his fingerprints should be on this," he said.

"Do orangutans even *have* finger-prints?" Ruth Rose asked.

Dink shrugged. "Whoever gave him the picture would have left *his* fingerprints, too."

"His trainer!" Josh said.

Ruth Rose nodded. "Yep. The orangutan might have taken the painting, but the real thief is the person who taught him how!"

CHAPTER 9

Uncle Warren was in the kitchen looking glum when Dink, Josh, and Ruth Rose rushed in.

"Forest Evans just called," Uncle Warren said. "He's coming back tomorrow! What will I tell him?"

Dink grinned. "Tell him we know who stole his painting!"

Uncle Warren nearly dropped his coffee cup. "Do you really know, Donny? Who?"

"The orangutan did it!" Josh said.

Interrupting each other, the three

kids told Dink's uncle what they thought had happened.

"But how would an ape recognize a valuable Monet?" Uncle Warren asked.

Dink unbuttoned his shirt and carefully placed the snapshot on the table.

"We think his trainer taught him to recognize the painting," Dink said.

His uncle studied the photograph. "It's Forest's painting, all right," he said. "And look, that's the Eiffel Tower in the background. This picture was taken in Paris!"

Uncle Warren shook his head. "I find this very hard to believe," he said. "An orangutan climbed up to my balcony, ate my oranges, then stole my friend's painting? Incredible!"

"Orangutans are very smart," Josh said. "I saw a nature program about them once. One orangutan learned to count. They taught another one to turn on a VCR and pop in a video!"

Uncle Warren nodded. "I'll give this photo to Detective Costello," he said.

"But how do we find the orangutan's owner?" Ruth Rose asked. "We don't even know his name."

"Wait a minute!" Dink jumped up and ran into the living room. He came back carrying the jeans he'd been wearing the night before.

"I took one of their flyers," he said, digging into the pocket. "Here it is!"

He opened the flyer and spread it on the kitchen table. In large block letters were the words:

FOWLERS' FARM

ANIMAL ACTS OF ALL KINDS

FOR PARTIES AND SCHOOL EVENTS

Below the words was a picture of

the man and woman they'd seen the night before. Their names were printed beneath the picture:

HARVEY AND GINNY FOWLER

Beside that picture was another one. In it, the orangutan was riding the pony. The caption said:

OLLIE THE ORANGUTAN
AND POLLY THE PONY!

At the very bottom of the page were a telephone number and address.

"They live in Ossining, New York," Dink's uncle said. "That's not far from here. Excellent, Donny!"

"Now all we have to do is get that detective to arrest them," Josh said.

"I'm afraid not," Uncle Warren said. "We have no proof that these people trained their animal to steal Forest's painting. We have a lot of theories, a photo, and hairs that *might* have come from that orangutan. Still, I doubt that's enough for Detective Costello to make an arrest."

"If only we could get Mr. or Mrs. Fowler's fingerprints," Dink said. "Then we could see if they match any of the prints on the snapshot."

"That would be a start," Uncle Warren said, "but still no proof that their animal stole the painting."

"What if we got a hair from Ollie?" Ruth Rose said. "If the hair matched the one we found in the kitchen, wouldn't that prove he was in this apartment?"

Dink's uncle smiled. "I think that would be enough to convince Detective Costello," he said. "But how do we obtain this hair?"

Ruth Rose grinned. "I thought you'd never ask," she said.

CHAPTER 10

Half an hour later, Uncle Warren handed Ruth Rose the telephone. "Good luck," he said.

"Don't worry," Josh said. "She's really good at tricking crooks!"

Ruth Rose smiled into the phone. "Hello, is this Mr. Harvey Fowler? My name is Ruth Rose. My birthday is tomorrow, and my parents want to hire Ollie and Polly. My father is Forest Evans, and he's very rich!"

Two minutes later, she hung up. "They're coming!" she said.

"Do you think Mr. Evans will mind if we use his property?" Dink asked.

His uncle beamed. "He'd love it! I can't wait to tell him when he returns from Europe."

"How will we get there?" Josh asked. "I've never even heard of Larchmont, New York."

"It's not far, Josh. I'll rent us a car," Uncle Warren said. "Now I have to make a few phone calls. This is going to be such fun!"

Early the next morning, Roger called to let them know the rental car was downstairs.

Ruth Rose was in disguise. She was wearing Uncle Warren's beret and a pair of his glasses.

"You look great!" Dink said. "Mr. Fowler will never remember you from the block party."

Uncle Warren and the kids went downstairs and climbed into the rental car. Dink's uncle drove them out of the city. They saw plenty of traffic and crossed a couple of bridges. Finally, Dink saw a sign that said:

WELCOME TO LARCHMONT

"Almost there," Uncle Warren said. "Forest has a beautiful home and a lot of land."

A few minutes later, he turned into a long driveway lined with trees. At the end of the driveway stood a large brick house. Behind it, Dink could see a pool and tennis courts.

"Awesome," Josh said.

"Yes, it's lovely out here," Uncle Warren said. "But I'd rather have people around me than trees."

He parked the car, and everyone got

out. Two men and a woman walked out of the garage.

Dink recognized Detective Costello but not the other two.

"This is Detective Rita Frost, my partner," Detective Costello said.

"And I'm Dr. Ted Parker," the other man said.

"Dr. Parker is the curator for primates at the Bronx Zoo," Detective Costello explained. "After the arrest, he'll take charge of the animals."

Detective Frost wore a blue dress and heels. She smiled at Ruth Rose. "Are you ready to act like a rich kid?" she asked.

"I'm a little nervous," Ruth Rose said. "What if the Fowlers recognize me?"

"I wouldn't worry about that," the woman said. "If what you've told us is true, they won't even look at you. He'll be thinking about how to break into this beautiful house."

"Okay, this is the plan," Detective Costello said. "Our backup car will let us know when the Fowlers drive in. Rita and I will pretend to be Mr. and Mrs. Evans. Ruth Rose is our daughter, the one who's having the birthday. Everyone else will stay in the garage until I give the word to come out. Any questions?"

Just then, the cell phone on Detective Costello's belt rang. He answered it, listened, then hung up.

"The Fowlers' trailer just entered the property," he said. "Inside, please, and no talking."

Dink, Josh, Uncle Warren, and Dr. Parker stepped into the garage.

"Good luck," Dink whispered to Ruth Rose.

Ruth Rose gave them a thumbs-up

as the garage door came down in front of her.

Two shiny black cars were parked inside the garage. Dink sat on the bumper of one of the cars. He could hear the trailer approaching. Then he heard car doors slamming and some muffled voices.

Josh had his ear to the garage door. He started to giggle when he heard Ruth Rose beg "Daddy" for a pony of her own.

"She gets to have all the fun," he whispered.

Dink gave Josh a nudge. "No talking!" Dink whispered back.

Josh lost his balance and backed into the wall, striking a button. Making a whirring sound, the garage door began to open.

CHAPTER 11

Dink felt himself blushing as everyone outside the garage turned to look at everyone inside.

The trailer stood a few yards away. Through a thick mesh screen, Dink saw Ollie and Polly.

"Say, what's going on here?" Harvey Fowler asked.

"Hey, wait a minute," his wife said. "They were at the block party! What's this all about, Mr. Evans?"

"I'm not Mr. Evans," Detective Costello said. He pulled his wallet out and flipped open his badge. "I'm Detective Frank Costello, New York City Police Department."

Detective Costello nodded at Dr. Parker, who walked over to the trailer. Dink watched him take out a pair of scissors and snip a few hairs from Ollie's arm. Then Dr. Parker went back into the garage.

Detective Frost took a plastic bag from inside her jacket. Through it, Dink recognized the Polaroid picture of the painting.

"I'm sure we'll find your finger-prints all over this photograph," she told Harvey Fowler. "Recognize it?"

Harvey Fowler glanced down at the picture. Dink saw his Adam's apple go up and down. "So? Big deal. What's wrong with having a picture? I've got lots of pictures."

"Trouble is, you have one picture

too many," Detective Costello said. "You taught your ape to steal the painting in this photograph."

Harvey Fowler smirked, showing a gold tooth. "I got one word for you: *proof.* You got any?"

Dr. Parker walked back to the group. "I think so," he said. "The hairs match. The ones I just snipped from Ollie are the same as the one found in Mr. Duncan's kitchen. They're both like the hair the kids found in front of the apartment building."

"Thank you, Dr. Parker," Detective Frost said. She looked at Harvey and Ginny Fowler. "You're both under arrest for grand theft."

"We didn't steal nothing and you can't prove we did!" Harvey Fowler yelled. "I can't help it if Ollie took some dumb painting."

"Give it up," sighed Ginny Fowler to her husband. "It's over."

She turned to Detective Frost. "Everything you said is true. Harvey's cousin works for an insurance company in Paris. Last week, he insured a Monet painting. When he saw that it was being shipped to New York, he took a snapshot and sent it to us. He also sent the address where the painting was going."

"Ginny, be quiet!" Harvey shouted. "We'll get outta this. I got another cousin who's a lawyer."

Mrs. Fowler ignored her husband. "Anyway, when Harvey saw the balconies on the back of Mr. Duncan's building, he trained Ollie to climb up there," she said. "The painting is hidden in the trailer."

Detectives Costello and Frost handcuffed the Fowlers. Then everyone walked over to the trailer.

It was divided in half. Ollie sat on one side, gazing out through the wire. On the other side, Polly stood munching hay. She didn't seem interested in what was going on in the human world.

"Where is it, exactly?" Detective Frost asked Ginny Fowler.

"There's a false bottom in Ollie's cage," Mrs. Fowler said. "You'll find a handle under the straw."

Detective Costello looked at Josh. "You want to climb in there, kid?"

Josh gulped. "Um, sure. He won't hurt me, will he?"

Ginny Fowler smiled at Josh. "Go ahead. Ollie likes kids."

Detective Frost opened the trailer's rear door and Josh crawled in. Ollie shuffled over and smelled Josh's hair.

Josh moved some of the straw and found a small, round handle. He tugged, and a part of the floor lifted up.

"It's in here!" Josh said.

Just then, a taxi pulled up next to the trailer. A short man with a brown beard stepped out. "Warren, who are all these people? What's going on?"

Uncle Warren shook Forest Evans's hand. "Welcome home, Forest. Make us a pot of tea, and we'll tell you the whole story!"

• • •

"What will happen to Ollie?" Ruth Rose asked. They were in the rental car. Dink's uncle was driving them back to the city. "He won't go to jail, will he?"

Uncle Warren shook his head. "Not at all. Dr. Parker will see that Ollie goes back to Borneo," he said. "There are special camps there where orangutans are taught to live in the wild again. Ollie will have a safe, happy life from now on."

"What about Polly?" Dink asked.

"She could be a problem," Uncle Warren said. "Dr. Parker hasn't been able to find anyone who wants a ten-year-old pony."

"I know someone who wants a ten-year-old pony," Ruth Rose said. "Me!"

"You?" Josh said. "Where will you keep her?"

"I don't know," Ruth Rose said. She nudged Josh with her elbow. "If only I knew someone with a barn!"

Josh laughed. "Oh, I get it. Okay, I'll ask my folks if Polly can live in our barn. But the twins will want to ride her."

"So will my little brother," Ruth Rose said. "We can all own Polly and we can all ride her!"

Josh leaned forward and patted Dink's head. "And Dinkus can clean out her stall!"

HAVE YOU READ ALL THE BOOKS IN THE

A to Z Mysteries®

SERIES?

Help Dink, Josh, and Ruth Rose . . .

...solve
mysteries
from A to Z!

Collect clues with
Dink, Josh, and Ruth Rose
in their next exciting adventure!

THE PANDA PUZZLE

The crowd quieted. Slowly, the mother panda moved into the sunlight. Her head swiveled around and she lifted her nose into the air. Suddenly she charged the fence and threw her body against the metal rails.

"What's wrong with her?" Ruth Rose asked.

A man unlocked the fence gate. Carefully, he crossed over to the cave, knelt down, and looked inside.

Then he reached in and pulled something out. To Dink, it looked like a round alarm clock. A small piece of paper was tied around it with a string.

"This is so weird!" Josh whispered. "What's going on?"

Irene stepped back to the microphone. Dink noticed her hand was shaking.

"This is a ransom note," Irene told the crowd. "Our baby panda has been kidnapped!"

Here's what kids, parents, and teachers have to say to Ron Roy about the **A TO Z MYSTERIES**® series:

"Whenever I go to the library, I always get an A to Z Mystery. It doesn't matter if I have read it a hundred times. I never get tired of reading them!" —Kristen M.

"I really love your books!!! So keep writing and I'll keep reading." —Eddie L.

"Keep writing fast or I will catch up with you!" —Ryan V.

"I love your books. You have quite a talent to write A to Z Mysteries. I like to think I am Dink. RON ROY ROCKS!" —Patrick P.

"Nothing can tear me away from your books!" —Rachel O.

"I like Dink the best because he never gives up, and he keeps going till he solves the mystery." —Matthew R.

"Sometimes I don't even know my mom is talking to me when I am reading one of your stories." —Julianna W.

"Your books are famous to me."
—Logan W.

"I think if you're not that busy, you could do every letter again." —Abigail D.

"I credit your books as one of the main influences that turned [my daughter] from a listener to a voracious reader."
—Andrew C.

"You have changed my third grader from an 'I'll read it if it is easy' boy into a 'let's go to the library' boy. Thank you so much, and please, keep up the great work."
—Kathy B.

"My third-grade students are now hooked on A to Z Mysteries! Thank you for sharing your talents with children and helping to instill in them a love for reading."
—Carolyn R.

A TO Z MYSTERIES® fans, check out Ron Roy's other great mystery series!

Capital Mysteries

#1: Who Cloned the President?
#2: Kidnapped at the Capital
#3: The Skeleton in the Smithsonian
#4: A Spy in the White House
#5: Who Broke Lincoln's Thumb?
#6: Fireworks at the FBI
#7: Trouble at the Treasury
#8: Mystery at the Washington Monument
#9: A Thief at the National Zoo
#10: The Election-Day Disaster
#11: The Secret at Jefferson's Mansion
#12: The Ghost at Camp David
#13: Trapped on the D.C. Train!
#14: Turkey Trouble on the National Mall

January Joker
February Friend
March Mischief
April Adventure
May Magic
June Jam
July Jitters
August Acrobat
September Sneakers
October Ogre
November Night
December Dog
New Year's Eve Thieves

If you like **A TO Z MYSTERIES**®,
take a swing at

BALLPARK®
Mysteries

#1: The Fenway Foul-Up

#2: The Pinstripe Ghost

#3: The L.A. Dodger

#4: The Astro Outlaw

#5: The All-Star Joker

#6: The Wrigley Riddle

#7: The San Francisco Splash

#8: The Missing Marlin

#9: The Philly Fake

#10: The Rookie Blue Jay

#11: The Tiger Troubles

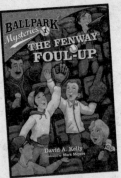